THIS BLOOMSBURY BOOK

BELONGS TO

....

For Andy Catchpole, with tons of thanks - SG

To Emma, with thanks - MT

First published in Great Britain in 2002 by Bloomsbury Publishing Plc
36 Soho Square, London, W1D 3QY
This paperback edition first published in 2003

Text copyright © Sally Grindley 2002
Illustrations copyright © Michael Terry 2002
The moral right of the author and illustrator has been asserted

A CIP catalogue record of this book is available from the British Library

ISBN 978 0 7475 6120 0

Printed and bound in China by South China Printing Co

3 5 7 9 10 8 6 4

The Sulky Vulture

Sally Grindley and Michael Terry

BLOOMSBURY
CHILDREN'S
BOOKS

'Eat your dinner,' said Boris's mum.

'Don't like meat,' said Boris.

'Then go without,' said Boris's dad.

Off stomped Boris with a 'Humph'.

Head pulled down, shoulders hunched up, toes curled in,
Boris the vulture is sulking.

'What's the matter, Boris?' asked Leo the leopard.

'I don't like meat,' said Boris.

'Never mind, Boris,' said Leo,
'let's have a game of chase.'

Leo chased Boris ... and caught him straightaway,
Boris chased Leo ... but Leo was too fast.

'I've had enough of this,' grumbled Boris.

Head pulled down, shoulders hunched up, toes curled in,
Boris the vulture is sulking.

'What's the matter, Boris?' asked Flora the zebra.

'I don't like playing chase,' said Boris.

'Never mind, Boris,' said Flora,
'let's play hide-and-seek.'

Boris hid behind a tree ... Flora found him straightaway. Flora hid in some grass ...

Boris couldn't find her though he
looked and looked and looked.

'I've had enough of this,'
he grumbled.

Head pulled down, shoulders hunched up, toes curled in,
Boris the vulture is sulking.

'What's the matter, Boris?' asked Tara the elephant.
'I don't like hide-and-seek,' said Boris.

'Never mind, Boris,' said Tara,
'let's throw coconuts.'

'Bet I can throw the furthest,' said Boris.

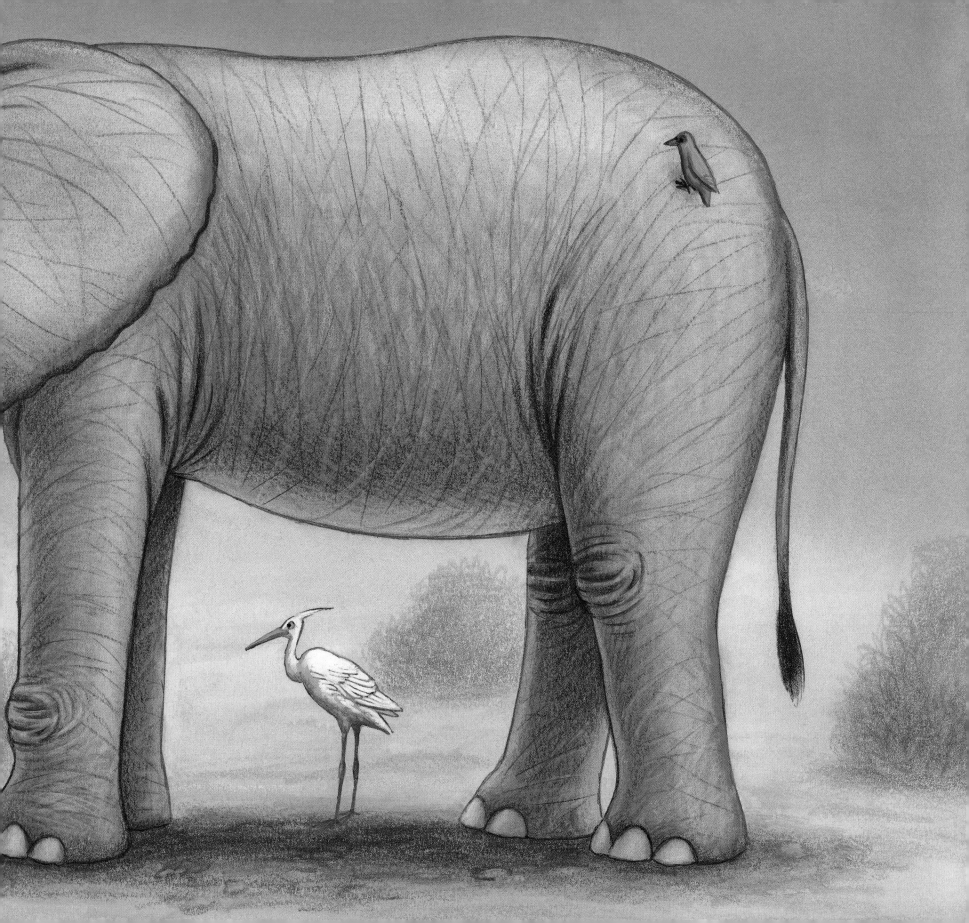

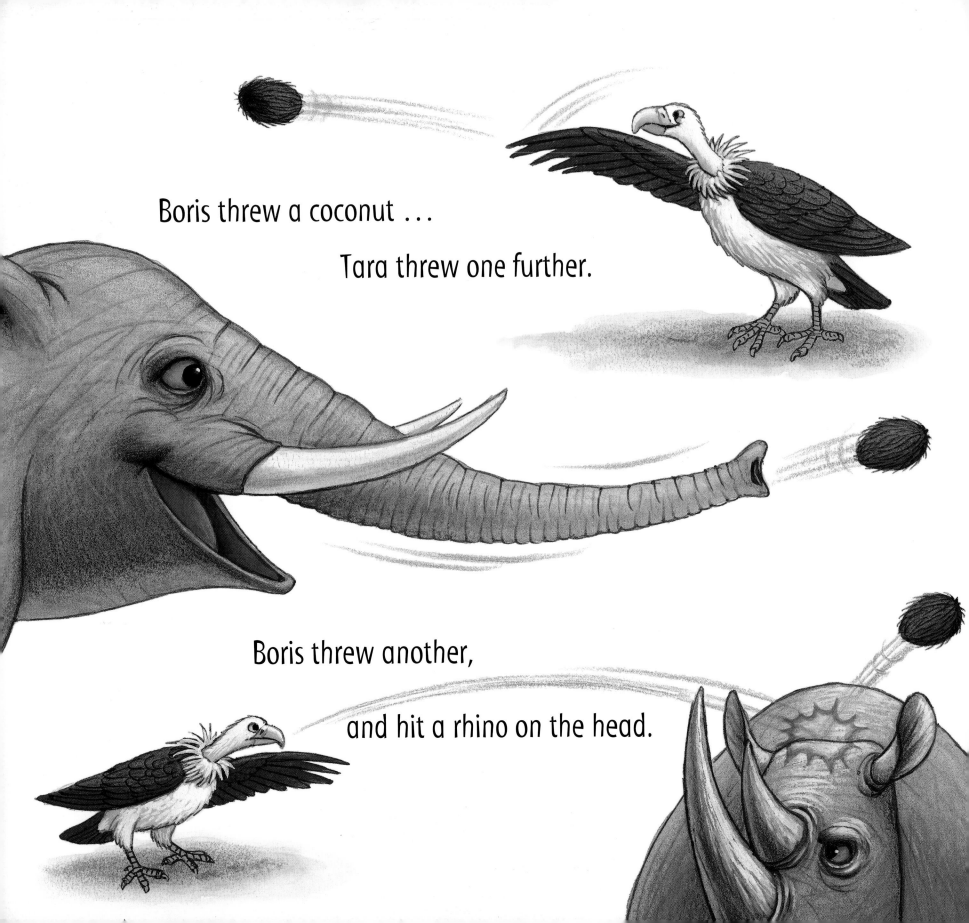

Boris threw a coconut ...

Tara threw one further.

Boris threw another,

and hit a rhino on the head.

The rhino CHARGED!
Boris leapt up into a tree ...

and the rhino JUST
missed him!

Head pulled down, shoulders hunched up, toes curled in,
Boris the vulture is sulking.

'What's the matter, Boris?' asked Marvin the baboon.
'I don't like rhinos,' said Boris.

'Never mind, Boris,' said Marvin,
'come and have a swing.'

Boris clambered on …
Marvin gave him a push.

Forwards Boris went …
and backwards again.

Forwards he went.
And backwards again.

'This is fun!' he cried.

And higher.

And higher.

Higher he went.

'Harder, push me harder!'

Marvin pushed him harder and ...

... the swing broke.

Head pulled down, shoulders hunched up, toes curled in,
Boris the vulture is sulking.

'What's the matter, Boris?' said Boris's mum.

'I don't like meat, and I don't like playing chase.
I don't like hide-and-seek and I don't like rhinos.
I don't like swings and — can I have a cuddle,
Mum?'

'Of course you can,' said Boris's mum.
'I'll give you a great big cuddle ...
and then it's time for bed.'

'But I don't like bed!' shouted Boris.

Enjoy more Bloomsbury books from Sally Grindley and Michael Terry ...

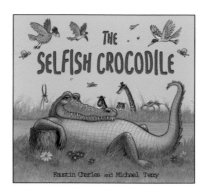

The Selfish Crocodile
Faustin Charles & Michael Terry

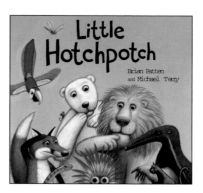

Little Hotchpotch
Brian Patten & Michael Terry

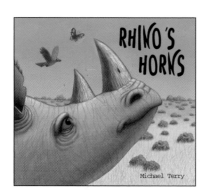

Rhino's Horns
Michael Terry

No Trouble At All
Sally Grindley & Eleanor Taylor

A New Room for William
Sally Grindley & Carol Thompson